The
Who Saved a Tree

story by
Robert N. McWilliam

illustrations by
John E. Rimmer

Chapter 1.

Brad Watson's face was so close to the ground that he was in constant danger of sneezing from the grass tickling his nose. Brad didn't want to sneeze. He was watching two large red ants pulling a bread-crumb through the grass toward their home. If he sneezed on them, the force of the sneeze would likely flatten the poor ants into the ground or at the very least blow the crumb away. Brad was fascinated by the efforts of the tiny animals: pushing, pulling, sometimes even lifting the morsel many times their size and weight.

"I wish I were that strong!" Brad thought to himself, flexing his muscles. A nine-year-old didn't have that much to flex!

He knew why the ants were so determined to move this prize to their anthill. With winter approaching, this would provide food for the colony for days. There was even more where this crumb had come from. Brad knew, because he was the one who had carefully placed the bread where the two foraging ants could easily find it.

Brad smiled, remembering their display of excitement when they discovered the food. What heroes they would be when they arrived at the hill! What tales they could tell their children!

Brad frowned. Did ants have children? He puzzled over this for a minute, then shrugged and made a mental note to ask his dad later. His dad was a biologist; he knew everything about animals.

Brad's stomach rumbled, telling him loudly that it was time for him to have a snack, just like those ants! He considered munching on a piece of the bread left in the bag, but then he remembered he hadn't spent all his allowance yet. He sat up and dug one grimy hand into a pocket of his shorts. Rummaging around, he withdrew his hand and carefully inspected its contents. A quarter, two nickels, a dime, and four pennies. His face brightened. That was enough for a candy bar at Mr. Edwards' general store, and a couple of jaw-breakers besides! A nice treat to start the long weekend!

Candy! Brad's mouth watered in anticipation. He loved candy! And Mr. Edwards had the best stuff in town! Brad jumped up and ran to the back door of his house. He pulled open the screen door and raced inside, dropping the bread bag on the kitchen table as he passed on his way to the front door.

"Going to the store, Mom!" he hollered toward the stairs where he knew his mother would be.

Mrs. Watson smiled at the shout and leaned over to look out the window of her study. Brad was already halfway down the block, his stomach's concentration driving his legs at top speed. She returned to her typewriter. Mrs. Watson was a freelance journalist for the town newspaper and right now she was struggling with an article for next week's edition.

By the time Brad had traveled six blocks, his pace had slowed to a fast trot. His running shoes slapped a rhythmic tattoo on the sidewalk as he leaned into a power turn at the corner and headed down the hill. There was the store now, straight ahead. As Brad approached, he slowed even more and scanned the yard behind the weathered grey building. His eyes widened with pleasure as he spied a small, bushy-tailed form among the multi-colored leaves covering the ground around a huge oak tree.

"Hi, Rufus!" he called out loudly as he hung over the top rail of Mr. Edwards' fence.

A grey squirrel popped up from the leaves at this sudden interruption and scampered to the safety of the tree. You may think that "Rufus" is a strange name for a grey squirrel, but Brad had first become acquainted with the furry creature in the early summer, when the coats of grey squirrels have a significant reddish tinge. As autumn approached, Rufus' coat had gradually assumed its characteristic silver-grey color, which would last all through the winter months. From his perch on a branch, Rufus spied Brad hanging on the fence rail and issued a brash and very annoyed scolding. Didn't this enormous creature know better than to bother him now? Winter was approaching and Rufus had only gathered half of the food his family would need to survive through the long, cold months.

Brad grinned as Rufus flashed down the trunk to the leaf-littered ground and picked up an acorn. Stuffing it into his cheek, Rufus quickly hopped to another nut, storing it in the same manner. Looking like a gopher with a terrible toothache, he ran swiftly back to the tree and climbed rapidly to a small hole halfway up the trunk. Peering over his shoulder at Brad far below, Rufus uttered one more string of squirrel-chatters designed to warn this intruder he'd be back. However, with his cheeks filled to bursting with nuts, not much sound reached the ground. Rufus dived into his den; Brad turned and dived through the side door of the store.

As always, Brad halted just inside the door and scanned the shelves. Sometimes Mr. Edwards brought in something new, and he and Brad had a standing bet as to whether Brad could spot it the first day it appeared. Carefully the boy peered at the brightly-colored displays, and then -- his eyes suddenly widened and a grin split his face from ear to ear. He marched up to the long counter, trying very hard to keep his delight from showing on his face. Casually, he inspected the huge round glass container full of jawbreakers sitting beside the cash register. Mr. Edwards looked up from his rolltop desk and smiled fondly.

"Hello, Bradley," he said, "How's my favorite customer this fine October afternoon?"

"Just fine, Mr. Edwards, sir," replied the boy, a smile beginning to tug at the corners of his mouth, "It sure is hot, isn't it? New teacher's sure giving us a lot of work. I've already used up the eraser Mom bought last summer. Think I'll tell her I'd like one of those new striped ones!"

Mr. Edwards chuckled and heaved himself gently to his feet. His friend didn't move as spryly as he used to, Brad thought, but he didn't think it was proper to let on.

"When was the last time I fooled you, Bradley?" mused the old storekeeper, "Seems my jawbreaker stock keeps going down, so it must have been a long time ago!"

He reached in the big jar and tossed an all-day black one in the air. Brad caught the large black orb expertly with his left hand and pushed it into his back pocket. The grin was still pinned on his face. Brad loved this game; Mr. Edwards was his favorite grown-up in the world, outside of his parents, of course.

"I came to get a candy bar, sir." Brad brought out his stash of coins and dropped them into the old man's grizzled palm. "I think there's enough for some more jaws too."

Mr. Edwards gravely counted the money, his bushy eyebrows pushing a dozen wavy wrinkles into his forehead. "Why, you're right, son! Pick out any bar you want, and we'll slip it in a bag along with a couple more slobbers!"

Mr. Edwards always called the big jawbreakers 'slobbers' because that's what happened when you tried to talk while sucking on one. Mr. Edwards always seemed to find a question to ask you at the right time, too! He'd chuckle when the black juice ran down your chin, and onto your shirt collar as well if you weren't quick!

Brad walked over to the candy shelves and began to inspect the wares offered there for his discerning eye. He'd already decided to get something different this time, and he wanted to carefully consider all the

12

choices before making up his mind. He was reading the description of the contents of the 'Coconut Cream Delight' when the bell over the front door tinkled and he looked up to see who the newcomer was.

It was Mrs. Finstead. Brad quietly hunkered down behind the shelves so she wouldn't see him. She always mussed up his hair and told him he was getting "sooo" tall whenever she spied him. He was lucky this time; Mrs. Finstead marched straight up to the counter, her face grim and full of those little lines around her mouth that Brad's dad called prissy.

Candy forgotten for the moment, Brad stared at the grey-haired lady. Mrs. Finstead was in a snit, that's for sure! Brad knew from experience that it was best to get very far away when this happened: Mrs. Finstead was liable to let loose on anyone in her path, and she surely did know some mean things to say!

"What's this I hear about your oak tree, Mr. Edwards?" she demanded in a booming voice, "Emma Sanford told me just this minute that you're fixing to cut it down!"

"Now, Mrs. Finstead," Mr. Edwards' voice was calm and soothing, "don't get yourself worked up. There's nothing I can do. My insurance agent told me he was going to have to double my premiums if I didn't get rid of it. He said there was too much risk of a tree that old falling over in a windstorm and landing on my store. I can't afford to pay that much. I have to cut down the tree."

"Risk, my Aunt Matilda!" Mrs. Finstead snorted, "All those pencil-pushers think about is money! What about history? What about our heritage? What about the beauty of our town? If you give in to this blackmail, who'll be next? There's a bigger tree right next to the butcher shop! And what about the one in the town square? Couldn't it fall over and kill someone sunning themselves in the park? Soon we won't have any trees, just a bunch of ugly stumps! Won't that look pretty?"

Mr. Edwards raised his hands placatingly. "Mrs. Finstead, I'm sorry, I really am, but I don't see any other choice. I've got to have insurance, and I can't afford the new rates. I'm afraid the tree will have to go."

Mrs. Finstead glowered angrily, and the two adults stood eye to eye for a long moment. Then the woman snorted again, pointed a long finger at the storekeeper, and spoke grimly.

"Mark my words, Mr. Edwards, you haven't heard the last of this! I'll not stand idly by and watch you destroy the beauty of our town, just for a little money!"

With that, she turned stiffly and marched out of the store, banging the door loudly behind her. Mr. Edwards sighed, shook his head wearily, and muttered something under his breath. He was about to return to his desk when he happened to catch sight of a small white face topped with tousled, reddish-brown hair peering at him over the counter.

"Sorry, Bradley, I forgot you were here, what with all that shouting. Have you chosen a candy bar yet?"

Brad's face was very long and his eyes were very large. "Mr. Edwards, you're not talking about the tree in back, are you? The oak tree?"

"Why, yes, son, that's the one. Why do you ask?"

"But, sir, that's where Rufus lives! He's been gathering nuts for weeks to carry him over the winter! It's too late for him to find a new home!" Brad's eyes began to fill with tears, and he quickly wiped at them with the back of his hand.

"Rufus? Who's Rufus?" queried the old man.

"The grey squirrel who lives in the tree," cried Brad, "He has a family and everything! You can't cut down his tree!"

Mr. Edwards came out from behind the counter and sat down in front of Brad. He pulled a large red handkerchief from his pocket and handed it gravely to the boy who took it and dabbed at his eyes before thrusting it back into the man's hand.

"I see you've made friends with Rufus," Mr. Edwards said gently, "and you're concerned about him.

Tell you what. I'll help you find him and his family a new home. How about that?"

"Where, Mr. Edwards? Where could they go? Rufus has always lived in your yard. It's his home! He doesn't know any other place to live! He wants to stay here!"

The tears began to stream down Brad's cheeks again, accompanied by a loud snuffling from his nose. Brad used the bottom of his shirt to pass over all the leaky areas this time as he continued to stare at his friend. Mr. Edwards' eyes were sad as he gazed worriedly at the miserable little boy.

"I don't know what else I can do, Bradley. I'm sorry."

Brad was silent, staring now at the worn wooden floor.

"How about you take your candy home and think on it? Here, I'll give you an extra slobber for free. Something will come to you, I'm sure. There has to be another home for Rufus."

"I don't much feel like any candy, sir," Brad said in a low voice, "Could I have my money back, please?"

Mr. Edwards twisted around to the cash register and picked the coins off the top. He handed them to Brad. Without a word, Brad turned and shuffled to the door, head hanging dejectedly. He slowly opened the door and pulled it softly closed behind him. Brad went home the long way, not wanting to see Rufus just now.

Chapter 2.

The next morning, Brad woke up early. He lay quietly in his bed, staring at the ceiling where his model airplanes swung on invisible threads. The autumn sun spread its rays gently over him, warming his cheek. Brad sat up in bed and threw off the covers. He knew what he had to do. His stomach churned at the thought, but his heart knew there were some things that a person had to stand up for.

Quickly the youngster dressed and tiptoed out of his room. It was Saturday, so his parents would be sleeping late. He didn't want to wake them, in case they tried to talk him out of what he was going to do. Right now Brad thought it wouldn't take much to talk him out of it.

He made his way out of the house and shut the front door quietly but firmly behind him. It was almost nine o'clock, so the store would soon be opening. He wanted to be there before any other customers arrived. Brad walked slowly along the route he had run with such happiness yesterday. What a difference one day can make! Finally he came to the fence by the big oak tree and leaned on it.

There was Rufus, rooting around in the leaves, searching for more acorns. He spied Brad and chattered loudly at him. Brad watched the squirrel rushing about on his tasks for a while. Then he took a deep breath and headed for the front of the store. As he came around the corner, he came face to face with Mr. Edwards, who was just unlocking the door. The storekeeper peered at him in surprise.

"Good morning, Bradley," he said, "You're up early today."

"Good morning, sir," replied Brad, "I came now because.... because there is something I have to say."

Mr. Edwards looked intently at the boy. He noticed the seriousness of Brad's expression and the stiffness in his shoulders. The old man sat down heavily in the old barrel chair beside the door and motioned the boy closer. Placing one hand softly on Brad's shoulder, he spoke gently.

"What is it, my boy?"

Brad took a deep breath and began to speak. "Mr. Edwards, you are one of my best friends. I spend a lot of time here with you, and I like you a lot. My dad knows I respect you because I'm always telling him things you say."

Mr. Edwards smiled and patted the boy's shoulder.

"But Rufus is my friend too. And he's in trouble. You say you're in trouble too, but I think losing your home is a lot worse trouble than paying more money. I can't be on your side and Rufus' side at the same time, and I think Rufus needs me more. And so I've decided I'm going to fight for Rufus. I'm only a kid, but I have to do whatever I can. Do you understand that?"

Mr. Edwards smiled sadly. "I do, Bradley. And I'm proud of you, proud to be your friend. You're a very wise young man."

Brad swallowed hard, trying to get rid of the gigantic lump that had appeared in his throat. He'd thought the worst was over, but what came next was very difficult to say.

"I thought about what I could do, and it didn't seem like it would be very much. I figured if I was going to fight for something I believe in, I might have to give up something. Sacrifice, my dad calls it. So, that's what I'm going to do."

Brad took another deep breath into his lungs. His hands twisted at the front of his shirt nervously. He shoved them deep into the pockets of his shorts.

"Mr. Edwards, until you promise not to cut down Rufus' tree, I'm not buying any more candy or anything else from you. And I'm going to ask my friends not to buy anything either, and my parents. And anyone else who will listen."

The words all came out in a rush. Brad finished, gulped at that stubborn lump in his throat and stared apprehensively at the old man. Mr. Edwards continued to look into the boy's eyes for a moment, then looked down and sighed deeply.

"I respect your beliefs, Bradley, and your courage. I'm sorry to hear your decision, but I don't see any way to change mine."

Mr. Edwards stood up, gazed solemnly at the boy, sighed again, and then turned and walked wearily into the store's interior, leaving Brad, now feeling very, very empty, behind on the step.

Chapter 3.

"Bradley, may I talk to you for a minute?"

Brad slid to a sudden halt on his way to his room. He gulped in a huge breath, and turned tensely toward the couch. Usually those words meant trouble for him. As he peered at his mother, he relaxed slightly. She didn't look angry; but with grown-ups you couldn't always be sure. Slowly Brad dragged himself over to her and stood with his head down, gazing at the toes of her shoes.

"Bradley, I was just down at Mr. Edwards' store. He said he wasn't so sure he should sell me any sugar until I spoke with you. What's going on?"

Brad finally raised his eyes and faced his mother's questioning gaze. He shifted his feet, ran one hand through his hair, folded his arms over his chest, then unfolded them, unable to speak past the pain in his throat. Sensing his agitation, Brad's mother gently pulled him onto her lap. Silently, she stroked his head, waiting for him to explain. Slowly, stumbling over the words, Brad began to tell the story. Once started, his voice strengthened, and the words burst out of him. As he finished, he stole a quick glance at his mother's face to gauge her reaction. He was surprised to see a tear in the corner of her eye. She quickly swiped at it with her hand and sniffed gently, bowing her head. Then she looked deeply into her son's face and ran her fingers through his unruly hair.

"Brad, I'm very proud of you for standing up for your friend and for what you believe in. Your father and I will support you in whatever way we can. If you need any help with anything, just come and ask, OK?"

"Thanks, Mom," replied Brad gravely, and he turned to run to his room. He had work to do.

Chapter 4.

"Hey, Brad! Whatcha doing?" The shout came from the street in front of the general store. Brad stopped writing and squinted his eyes against the noon-time glare of the hot sun. On the street, on his battered bright-red imitation-official dirt bike, was Brad's best friend, Oscar Nordstrom. Oscar was about the skinniest kid you've ever seen. Widely-known as 'Beanpole', most people looked behind him for a shadow! His arms and legs were as big around as a broomstick, and his neck not much more. Brad noticed a few new cuts and scratches as well as a large bandaid on Oscar's bare leg, but wasn't surprised. Oscar was absolutely fearless. The condition of his bike hadn't happened by accident; no sir, it happened from being ridden off bigger hills, over knottier logs, down steeper ramps, and into more walls than any other bike in town.

Other kids spoke wide-eyed and in whispers about Oscar's skill with a bike. They came from all over town to watch him perform.

Oscar dropped his bike carelessly in the dust of the road and bounded up to the sidewalk in front of Brad. A wide grin split his freckled face from ear to ear. The brightest, sharpest blue eyes Brad had ever seen appraised him and then moved to the sign Brad was diligently working on. One eyebrow rose as his eyes scanned the hastily-crayoned words. He read aloud, stumbling a bit. Oscar wasn't known for his reading skills.

"'HELP RUFUS. SAVE THE TREE.' What's this about?"

Brad quickly filled him in on the details. Oscar knew Rufus too. He spent almost as much time as Brad hanging over the fence.

Oscar's face lit up. "Can I help? Where's my sign?"

Brad pointed to the fire hydrant near the corner of the store. A number of flat sticks attached to large pieces of stiff cardboard leaned there. A package of crayons lay beside them in the shade. Oscar rushed over, pulled out one sign and grabbed a crayon as he flopped down onto the sidewalk and held the sign on his knees. His forehead scrunched up in concentration for a few seconds, then he yipped excitedly and bent

to work. A minute later he flung down his crayon and sprang to his feet, brandishing his handiwork for Brad to read.

"'DON'T CUT THE TREE. LEAVE IT FOR THE BEAVERS!'"

Brad frowned. "There aren't any beavers here!"

"Exactly!" crowed Oscar, "That means it'll never get cut down!"

Brad wasn't so sure about Oscar's logic, but he wasn't going to turn down the help. As he smiled and nodded enthusiastically, Oscar bounded over to solemnly fall into line behind him. Together they marched up and down in front of the store all afternoon. Many people came by, some walking, some on bikes, others in their cars. Everyone was curious about their mission. Some applauded and left without buying anything; some went in anyway, excusing themselves by saying it was too far to the other store, and besides, it didn't have as good a selection. Brad gazed sadly at each one of these folks; he knew they didn't understand about Rufus, or maybe even about trees.

At about three o'clock, Brad's mother came by with a jug of ice-cold lemonade. Were the two lads ever thirsty! They each finished off two large glasses almost as fast as they were filled!

Brad groaned. "My feet hurt, Mom."

Debra Watson looked sympathetically at her son. "Do you want to quit and come home?" she asked softly.

Brad sat bolt upright. "No!" he said firmly, "I can't quit! How would Rufus feel? Come on, Oscar. Let's get back to work."

Oscar rolled his eyes at Brad's mother, but obediently got to his feet and picked up his sign. The lemonade jug and glasses vanished into the Watson car. Brad's mom waved as she left; the two boys resumed their vigorous marching back and forth along the sidewalk, refreshed by their snack.

About half an hour later the first sign of trouble appeared. By this time, Brad had picked up a new recruit: Jamie Rodriguez, whose family had only recently moved from Brazil. Jamie was a short, spindly kid, with long thick black hair that was always falling over his eyes. Brad thought Jamie probably pushed that hair back a thousand times a day! Jamie knew a lot about trees, and why it was important not to cut them down. It had to do with a gas in the air called carbon dioxide, Jamie told them, and anyone else who came by. Trees breathe carbon dioxide like we breathe oxygen and they help to keep the air clean for us. If there were no trees, there would be too much carbon dioxide, and we couldn't live. Jamie also told them about all the strange and mysterious birds and animals that made their homes in the trees in Brazil.

Brad thought Rufus would like to meet some of those creatures, as long as they didn't take any of his winter food! Jamie's sign said:

'BE FAIR, SHOW YOU CARE, SAVE
THE TREE AND HELP OUR AIR.'

Jamie was a bit of a poet. Brad was glad. The new sign attracted a lot of attention.

The trouble showed up in the form of Reggie Peterson. Reggie fancied himself as stronger and smarter than everybody else his age; everybody else thought he was just bigger and cockier, and dumb to boot. It was easy to get around Reggie, if you didn't confront him head-on, that is. All you had to do was pretend you were scared (which wasn't hard, most times!), and Reggie would swagger away, crowing about another victory.

"So here are the three tree-huggers I've been hearing about!" Reggie sneered as he advanced on the smaller boys, who responded by becoming very quiet and backing away in a huddle. "Who do you think you are, you little do-gooders! Save a tree! Ha! Cut it up for firewood, I say! My old man would be glad to have the free wood, I bet. I think I'll go right home and tell him!"

His glance fell on the signs, and he scanned them quickly, breaking into loud chortles of laughter. "Artists, too, eh? What a bunch of crap! Maybe if I tear them up, you can do better next time!"

His confident advance toward the three came to a sudden halt as he was confronted with the pointed ends of three sign-holders. Reggie paused, then shrugged and started to turn away. Quick as a flash, as the three other boys relaxed, he swung back and sprang at Brad, wresting the stick from his grip. He laughed, holding Brad's sign over his head. "Guess I showed you! No match here for Reggie Peterson!" His arms began their downward arc, with Brad's prize sign hurtling to its destruction. Three sets of wide eyes watched in horror. Suddenly the sign stopped. Reggie stood frozen, his face contorted with a look of fear and pain. The three looked at each other in confusion. What on Earth was happening? Then they heard a soft voice, apparently coming from empty air.

"Put it down gently, there's a good boy." The voice was female, with a slight drawl and rich tones that Brad recognized immediately.

"Millie!" he cried joyfully, and rushed forward to rescue his sign. His two cohorts crowded in as Reggie

turned toward the road, his neck caught in the iron grip of five long black fingers. The most beautiful fingers he had ever seen, Brad decided right there. The fingers belonged to Millie Sanford, ten years old and the only kid in town who could face Reggie Peterson down and make him eat dirt. The fingers let go abruptly, but Reggie's relief was short-lived. A sandaled black foot planted itself firmly in his backside and pushed! Reggie took a flying leap into the dusty street, accompanied by hoots and jeers from the sidewalk. He sprawled face first in the dirt, and came up spitting and mad as an old tomcat. When he saw Millie regarding him confidently from the sidewalk, clenched hands resting on her hips, he paused and brushed off his pants.

"Getting girls to do your fighting now, eh? Pretty brave bunch! Who cares about your stupid signs anyway? Nobody is going to listen to you! You're just kids!" He turned and ran down the street, but only for a few yards. Then he remembered who he was, and settled into his usual swaggering walk. The boys watched to make sure he was safely away, and then collapsed to the curb. Millie lowered herself daintily to join them, tucking her long legs under the edge of the boardwalk. She examined her freshly-painted fingernails closely, a satisfied smile curving her lips, revealing a set of perfect, sparkling white teeth.

"Thanks, Millie," said Brad, and the others echoed his sentiments, "We were in real trouble."

"That ole boy?" snorted the girl, "He's nothin' but an old mongrel dog! Lots of bark, but not very much bite!" Her long braids swung around her face as she spoke, and her large brown eyes flashed angrily. "Ah came over to help y'all when my mother told me what you was doing. Ah want to carry a sign too and help save the tree." Millie's way of talking fascinated Brad. Her words seemed to be made of rubber, and she stretched them to the maximum!

"Great! Sure! Yeah!" The boys' enthusiasm rang through the air as the boys tumbled over each other to fetch a sign for Millie.

What to put on it? All four sat in silent concentration. Then, Millie straightened, smiling widely. "Ah've got it!"

She bent to work, crayon gripped lightly in her long graceful fingers, moving in long fluid strokes over the paper. The boys watched intently as a beautiful picture emerged. All three loudly voiced their appreciation.

"Wow! That's incredible! How'd you learn to draw like that?"

The paper Millie held up with shyly grinning pride revealed a remarkable likeness of Rufus himself, perched outside his nest-hole and peering out at the

world with a look of intense pleading on his whis-kered face.

"That's perfect!" said Brad.

"It's awesome!" added Oscar, and Jamie nodded in agreement.

"You will be at the front of our line," said Brad, and they scrambled up to resume their march.

Chapter 5.

The next day, the four crusaders were back marching as Mr. Edwards arrived to open up. His eyebrows rose significantly higher as he noted the increase in the ranks of his opponents and the messages on their signs. He greeted them all gravely by name, and the four all responded in kind. Then the storekeeper vanished inside, and the children resumed their task.

Back and forth they marched, hour after hour, broken only by lemonade breaks provided by willing parents, glowing with pride in their children. In the middle of the afternoon, a sign appeared in the front window of the store. The four kids crowded around it:

'SALE! ALL ITEMS 25% OFF!'

Four faces exchanged wordless glances, then back to the line they went, more determined than ever. They knew they were having an effect; Mr. Edwards was definitely losing business. But now they would have to work even harder: a sale attracted many people.

And it did. Twice as many potential customers approached the store, only to be confronted by four very serious and determined youngsters eager to explain their position.

"You kids ought to have a petition!" one lady said, and explained when her words brought blank stares. Immediately a call went out for paper, and soon signatures were appearing with regularity on the hastily-constructed petition form. At four o'clock, a large shadow fell across the picket line, and everyone, including three or four watching or chatting bystanders, stopped to gaze silently at the newcomer. A very tall, and very, very wide man in a black suit stood in the road blocking the sunlight. Because of his position, he appeared as a massive and somehow menacing mountain looming over them. Then the man moved up onto the sidewalk and plunked himself down in the big barrel chair. The chair groaned in protest, but it decided to hold together, at least for now, though it continued to emit squeaks and screeches every so often.

The man looked impassively at the four youngsters for a long moment, then suddenly cleared his throat loudly. "Harrumph!"

Brad jumped, and so did the others, with the exception of Millie, who surveyed the intruder with disdain.

"Now then," the man's voice matched his size. It boomed out of him like a big brass bell, causing them all to retreat a step. "What's all this nonsense? What are you kids hoping to prove with this display of foolishness?"

"Excuse me, sir," came Brad's quavering voice, "but who are you?"

The man turned his large dark expressionless eyes on the small boy and said nothing for a long moment. Brad fidgeted uncomfortably. Taking off his rimless spectacles, the man wiped them slowly with a huge white handkerchief pulled from a jacket pocket. After replacing them, he moistened his lips with his tongue and addressed Brad directly.

"Are you the leader of this crew, young man?" he boomed.

Brad gulped. "Yes sir," he stammered, "Bradley Watson, sir. These are my friends Millie Sanford, Jamie Rodriguez, and Oscar Nordstrom. We are trying to save our friend Rufus' home. He doesn't want to move."

"Humph," was the response followed by another long stare.

Oscar pushed forward. "You know our names now. What's yours?" Oscar stood his ground in the face of a bushy-browed frown, although Brad could see the muscles in his friend's skinny legs poised for flight if need be.

"Mr. Norman Tuttle, at your service." A business card appeared like magic in Tuttle's large hairy hand. Oscar grabbed it from him, and held it up so the others could read. Mr. Tuttle watched in silence. Brad looked up first.

"Insurance?" he said, "Are you the man who insures Mr. Edwards' store?"

"That's correct, young man," was the reply, "and I've come here to see what all the fuss is about and get this situation cleared up so my client can get back to his business. After all, how can an honest, hard-working man like Mr. Edwards expect to keep his family fed and a roof over their heads if you're driving away his customers?"

"You mean, how can he pay your insurance fees, don't you, MR. Tuttle?" Millie put some kind of emphasis on the word "Mister", as though questioning whether it really belonged to him.

"You watch your tongue, girl," boomed the big man, his voice becoming darker and more threatening. He thrust his heavy jaw toward her belligerently. "What have you got to do with this trouble anyway?"

"Seems to me there wouldn't be no trouble without your new insurance rates, Mr. Tuttle." Millie backed

off a bit on her tone. No sense getting the enemy too riled up before you found out his weak spots.

"Nonsense," Tuttle said, "My rates are the fairest in the valley! I have to protect my clients! What if that tree fell down in a windstorm and we didn't have enough money to pay out all the claims? We've got to protect ourselves, that's all I can say."

"Ain't no trees ever fell down in this town that I know of."

Brad twisted around and looked for the owner of this new voice. It was an ally, and a strong one, by the sound of it.

So did Mr. Tuttle. He fixed the newcomer with a steely glare. "Who might you be, sir?" The menace was back in his voice.

"Homer Bledsoe is my name," came the reply, and the speaker shouldered his way through the rapidly-growing crowd. Homer had white hair, long and flowing, with a brown, lined, grizzled face that Brad bet had seen a hundred summers.

"I've lived in this valley for seventy-five years, and the only trees I've ever seen fall in a wind are those left unprotected and alone in the fields. And none of those was oak!" Blue eyes as intense as Oscar's flashed with the words.

"You some kind of expert on trees, Mr. Bledsoe?" queried the insurance man in a soft voice. Brad didn't like this new voice. The other might be loud and booming, but at least it was honest. This one seemed sly, somehow.

"No, sir, I'm just a very good observer. And I have an excellent memory."

"Two admirable qualities, I'm sure, Mr. Bledsoe, but not sufficient for the task at hand. I have had forestry experts evaluate this tree, and they have assured me there is significant structural weakness to justify my insurance rates."

"May we ask who these experts are, Mr. Tuttle?" asked Homer.

"Certainly. I have nothing to hide. These men are well-qualified and well-known in this town. They are the owners of the furniture factory here, Jackson Bauer and Miles Hanson."

A murmur of laughter with an undercurrent of anger rippled through the crowd. "Those two are just out for themselves," someone shouted. "They want the wood!"

Mr. Tuttle heaved himself abruptly to his feet, and the four children and the bystanders fell back in sudden silence.

"No matter," boomed Tuttle, "I am satisfied and that's that. The tree comes down tomorrow." With those words, he turned and strode into the store, banging the screen door shut behind him.

The crowd shuffled about for a few minutes, growling to itself, and then slowly and gradually dispersed. One lady patted Brad on the head, saying "You did your best, son!"

The four crusaders sat down dejectedly on the sidewalk and stared glumly at each other. "What are we going to do?" whispered Jamie. "What's Rufus going to do?"

"We'll think of something!" said Brad resolutely, "Let's go home now and meet in the morning. Maybe something will happen."

"Yeah, like Mr. Tuttle getting hit by lightning!" Oscar crowed. They all looked hopefully at the sky. Unfortunately, there was not even a hint of a cloud, let alone a storm.

After everyone left, Brad trudged glumly to the back of the store, and leaned on the fence. Rufus was perched on a branch, quietly watching the boy.

"What am I going to do, Rufus?" Brad whispered.

Chapter 6.

When Brad opened his eyes the next morning, the patch of sky he could see through his bedroom window was grey and cloudy. "Perfect weather to kill a tree." he said gloomily. He lay still, his covers pulled up to his chin. Suddenly, his eyes widened and he sprang out of bed, bare feet thumping on the rug and then down the stairs as he rushed to the telephone.

Within a few minutes, he had contacted his three friends and excitedly explained his plan. He scampered back to his room to dress, then rocketed downstairs again and headed for the front door.

"Whoa there, young man!" his father's strong arms swept Brad off his feet, "Where are you off to so early?"

"Let me go, Dad," protested the boy, struggling to free himself, "I've got to meet my friends! We have a plan to save Rufus and his tree!"

John Watson set his son on the floor and squatted down to meet his eyes. "Brad, I know you've worked really hard to save Rufus' home. I'm very proud of you for all you have done. But, son, maybe it's time to give up. I hear the people are coming today to cut down the tree. Not all battles can be won, no matter how right the cause is. I don't want you to get hurt. Perhaps it would be better if you didn't go around the store today."

"No, Dad!" Brad said firmly, "I have to try one more thing! I've already talked to my friends, and they're all meeting me there. Please, Dad! I have to do this! Rufus is counting on me! I can't let him down!"

Tears chased each other down Brad's cheeks as he pleaded with his father. Mr. Watson looked searchingly into his son's eyes. Finally, he sighed deeply and bowed his head.

"All right, Bradley, you can go," he said, "but on one condition: Your mother and I want to be there in case of trouble."

"Thanks, Dad!" Brad gave his father a mammoth hug, "Okay if I meet you there? The guys are waiting."

John Watson smiled and waved Brad on his way. The young boy tore out of the house and sped down the street. His father watched him go with tears of his own sparkling his eyes. Boys grew up so quickly these days, he thought.

Chapter 7.

As fast as Brad ran, his mind was moving even quicker. He was going over The Plan, making sure he hadn't forgotten any important details. He hoped Oscar had been able to find all the equipment.

Rounding the corner, Brad spotted his friends waiting expectantly by the fence. They started to wave as soon as he appeared. No one else was in sight; no cars, trucks, or tree-cutting machines occupied the street. It was just like any other ordinary day.

"Did you get them, Oscar?" panted Brad as he skidded to a stop, gasping for breath.

Oscar grinned and reached into his shorts' pocket. There was the sound of clinking metal as he revealed......four pair of shiny official Dick Tracy handcuffs!

"Good work!" said Brad, pounding his friend on the back. "Now let's get in there before anyone comes along and stops us!"

The four children tumbled over the fence and ran quickly to the tree. Arranging themselves around the massive trunk, they attached the manacles to their wrists. A human chain now encircled the tree, the four youngsters facing outward, waiting nervously for what would happen next.

A sudden loud chattering made all four jump and peer upwards. A large pair of inquiring black eyes, topped with inquisitive grey-haired ears, regarded them solemnly from a hole in the trunk. A thickly-whiskered nose sniffed curiously at the strange sight below.

"Rufus!" called Brad, "Don't worry! We're going to protect you! No one will cut down your home now!" The squirrel chattered again, swishing his bushy tail in what the children were sure was approval and gratitude for their efforts.

Another noise cut across the early-morning silence. Four heads swung around to look out at the street. Jamie and Oscar couldn't see very well, since they were behind the tree, but a little tugging and stretching gave them a view too. The sound was definitely a motor, a big one by the deep-throated

growl of it. Probably the tree-cutters' truck! Brad took a deep breath.

"Everybody ready?" he asked. Three nervous voices answered affirmatively. "Okay, let's join hands so they can't see the cuffs." Hands fumbled for each other, trying to conceal the shine of metal. They waited, hearts thundering in their young chests.

With a squeal of brakes and a swirl of dust, a large yellow truck pulled to a stop beside the fence. A man's face peered at them, mouth hanging open in astonishment at the sight confronting him. Then he jumped out of the cab, hollered to someone out of sight, and strode over to the fence, his wide eyes taking in the scene. The four youngsters remained silent, staring steadily at the man. Rufus chattered defiantly. The dust cloud slowly settled. Silence descended once more, as though the whole world held its breath. Not even a bird could be heard.

Fear clutched at Brad's stomach. He'd known this was going to happen, but he was scared to the soles of his runners anyway. The figure that had just appeared on the sidewalk was none other than Mr. Norman Tuttle!

Brad drew a ragged breath. He felt Millie's fingers squeeze his hand encouragingly. Glancing at her, Brad saw the determination in her stare right at the big man, and his spirits rose. 'We can beat him,' he whispered to himself, 'I just have to be strong.' Rufus chattered again, and Brad's resolve strengthened.

"You can't cut down this tree!" he shouted defiantly, "We won't let you!" The others took up the cry, and the men were silent, obviously taken aback by this unexpected event. Tuttle and the other man conferred briefly, then the driver left at a run while Tuttle turned to look angrily in the direction of the children. His voice boomed across the grassy space between them.

"You kids are breaking the law, you know," he shouted, "Trespassing is a serious offence!"

There was a momentary pause as the four digested this news, then Millie shouted back, "It's Mr. Edwards' property! Only he can complain about us!"

"Yah!" taunted Oscar, and the other boys joined in.

Mr. Tuttle smiled grimly. "That's why I've sent for him. And the sheriff! This tree is coming down today, and that's it!" He leaned against the top rail of the fence, a smile of satisfaction spreading over his face. The children shuffled uneasily, and waited in silence.

All at once, a number of sounds broke the stillness: screeching tires, wailing sirens, excited voices. A group of people appeared from around the side of the store. The children straightened, trying to identify individuals, hoping for some friendly faces. There was Mrs. Finstead, waving her handkerchief at them and shoving Mr. Tuttle out of her way. There was Millie's mom, and Jamie's big sister, and Homer Bledsoe. Brad felt better, seeing all those people out there. Looking for his parents, he spotted them at the edge of the crowd. Now everything would be fine; his mom and dad wouldn't let anything happen to him. You see, Brad might be acting pretty brave right now, but he was after all only nine years old!

Mr. Edwards pushed his way to the front of the noisy, milling crowd and everyone gradually became silent. Mr. Edwards gazed at Brad, and Brad looked right back at him. Neither spoke. Brad thought the old man looked very sad.

Another figure pushed its way forward, and the crowd murmured in anticipation. Brad's heart seemed to stop for a long, long time. Sheriff Jackson T. Booker glared at him fiercely, pulling at the big leather belt wrapped around his large rounded middle. The crowd seemed to melt back as the sheriff bellowed at the children. Mr. Tuttle's booming voice was a whisper compared to Sheriff Booker's!

"YOU KIDS COME OUT OF THERE RIGHT NOW!" he hollered, and so compelling was his voice that Brad took a step forward. He was brought up short by the handcuffs, and then by the scornful look Millie threw at him. Face burning with shame, he gathered his courage and shouted back.

"We're not coming out! We're going to stay here until you promise not to cut down the tree!"

"Enough of this nonsense!" the sheriff growled, "Danny! Get in there and get those kids away from that tree!"

A uniformed young man with a deputy's badge pinned to his shirt vaulted the fence in one easy motion and sauntered toward the tree. Brad looked up into his face and shrank back against the rough bark. Deputy Danny Green smiled and said, "Okay, let's go now. Don't give me any trouble!" He reached to take Brad's arm and pull him away from the tree. A frown creased his forehead as he encountered resistance. He bent to look more closely at Brad's arm. A grin of admiration appeared, and he looked at Brad with new respect.

"Sheriff, they've gone and handcuffed themselves to each other!" he called back to the group at the fence. A cheer went up from the onlookers, and a round of applause followed. Sheriff Booker, Mr. Tuttle, and Mr. Edwards did not join in, although Brad thought he saw the trace of a smile on Mr. Edwards' face. Then Mr. Tuttle was pulling at the storekeeper's arm and

leading him away, and Brad lost sight of him. The sheriff was trying, without much success, to calm the crowd, which was growing larger by the minute. Notes of anger and frustration seemed to be creeping into their voices, too, as they shouted and gestured at the lawman. Then there was a brief struggle as someone forced his way to the front. It was Mr. Tuttle, wearing a triumphant smile and brandishing a large pair of wirecutters! He tossed them to Deputy Green, who approached the four children once again, and apologetically motioned to Brad.

"All right now, Brad," he said, "Hold out your hand so I can get that cuff off of you. I don't want to pinch you with these cutters!"

"Don't you do it, Brad!" yelled Oscar from the other side, "My brother will whip me if his cuffs get broke!"

"Think of Rufus!" hollered Jamie, and Millie kept jerking her hand around so Deputy Green couldn't get hold of the chain in his cutters.

The crowd was getting really worked up now. Cries of "Child beaters!" "Police brutality!" "Money grubbers!" "Tree-haters!" filled the air, and a lot more besides. Then, without warning, the noise ceased, and Deputy Green looked around to see what had happened. The four children peered anxiously around him.

On the top rail of the fence was Mr. Edwards, holding up his arms for silence. Everyone looked expectantly at the old man who shook with emotion as he waited for complete attention.

"I've lived in this town for fifty-seven years," he began, scanning the faces around him, "the last thirty of those running this store. I've always tried to be fair in my dealings with the people here. I've always felt people are more important than things. But there is something more important than people." He swung slowly around to face Brad and his friends. "Courage. Ideals. Beliefs. The strength to take a stand, to risk being laughed at, to risk being hurt, and to risk yourself for a friend."

Mr. Edwards climbed slowly over the fence, John Watson materializing at his side to lend him a hand. The old man walked over to the tree and gently laid a hand on Brad's shoulder. He turned to face the crowd.

"I've been blind for this last week. Blind to those signs of character in these children. Blind to what's important. That's over now." Mr. Edwards straightened himself and looked squarely at Mr. Tuttle. "You can take your tree-cutters and go home, Norm. I won't be needing them. Send me the invoice for my new insurance rate. This tree is staying!"

A cheer burst from the crowd. The four children added their joyous voices, victory shining in their eyes. Mr. Edwards turned and thrust out his hand to Brad, then burst out laughing when the young man's hand was brought up short by the restraining handcuff.

"Who's got the keys for these contraptions?" he chuckled.

Brad twisted to look at Oscar. His friend's face was covered by a look of intense pain and embarrassment. "I'm a dead man!" he groaned. "I think I lost the keys on the way over!"

Mr. Edwards doubled over with laughter. He motioned to Deputy Green. "Looks like you get to use that bolt-cutter after all, Danny! Oscar, tell your brother I personally will see to it he gets four new sets.....with keys!"

Brad shook Mr. Edwards' hand solemnly, then rushed in and delivered a powerful hug to the old man. As he stepped back, John Watson appeared, squeezing his son's shoulder, pride evident in his eyes.

"Tom," he turned to the storekeeper, "I've just been speaking to some of the other townspeople here, and we have a proposition for you. Because we believe this tree is now a symbol of our community, we want to open a "Tree Preservation Fund" to help raise the extra

money. I've already collected fifty dollars! And you'll never guess who the first donation came from!?"

"Who, Dad?" Brad burst out excitedly.

"Why, Mr. Norman Tuttle, that's who!" his father responded with a wide grin.

"How about that!" chuckled Mr. Edwards, "Just goes to show: you never can tell about people!"

"Maybe he heard what you said about what was important, Mr. Edwards," said Brad, holding tightly to his friend's hand.

"Maybe he did, son. Maybe he did."

A loud chattering from above startled them. Everyone looked up to see Rufus regarding them from his perch, his bushy tail swishing back and forth.

"I think Rufus agrees with you, Mr. Edwards!" said Brad.

"I think he's thanking you," responded the old man.

"See you later, Rufus!" called Brad as the group of happy tree-savers made their way toward the store. Even though it was a holiday, and the store officially closed, Mr. Edwards felt a round of free jawbreakers wasn't out of line today.

Brad smiled. It had turned out to be a good day after all. A very good day indeed.

The End

Rob and John both grew up in small towns, John in Alberta and Rob next door in Saskatchewan. Rob divided his time between collecting rocks and fossils, and staring at the stars, while John was more likely to be found mesmerized by the roar of the drilling rigs in his backyard.

Both have kept their feet firmly on the ground, Rob as a geologist and John as a driller, but they also both developed a fascination with space: Rob's favorite astronaut is Harrison Schmitt, the last person to walk on the Moon, who was also a geologist! John's is Bruce Willis, in the movie *Armageddon*, because he too was a driller! John's favorite movies include *Ice Age, Up, The Life and Times of Mickey Mouse*, and any other animated movies he can lay his hands on, while Rob can be found watching *Jurassic Park, Lord of the Rings, Journey to the Center of the Earth*, and all of *Star Trek* and *Star Wars*.

John's talent with drawing came to Rob's notice when they met at SAIT in Calgary, sometime in the last millennium. That led to their collaboration on this project. More could be in the works too. Rumors are the next book could be about........ What? It's still a secret? Sorry, can't tell you! Stay tuned!!!